S eepy Me

Sleepy Me

by
Marni McGee

illustrated by
Sam Williams

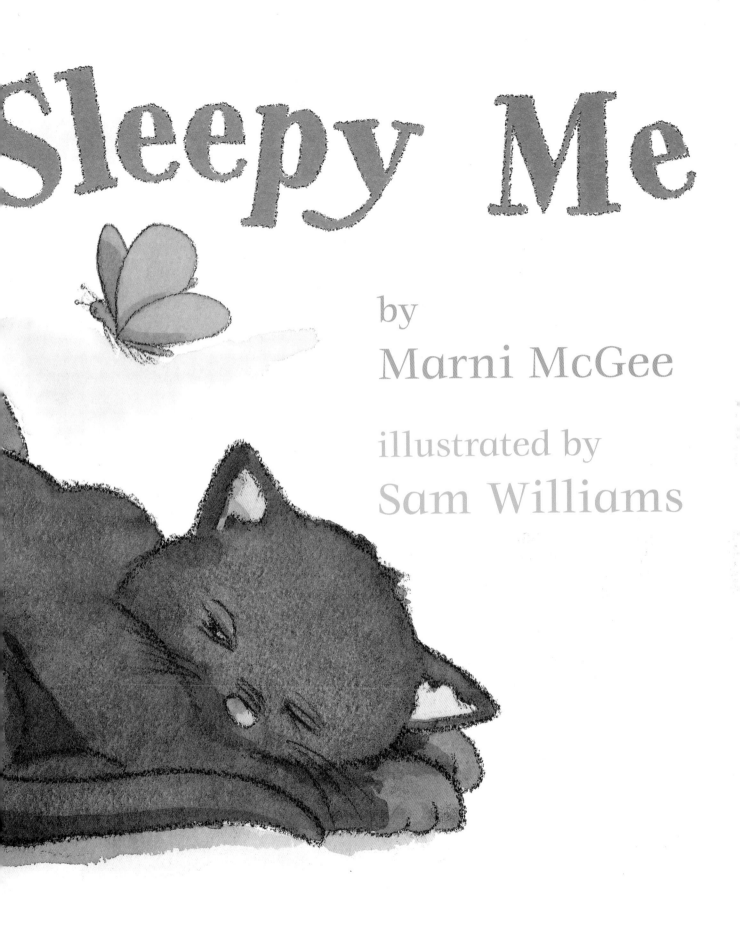

MACMILLAN CHILDREN'S BOOKS

First published in the United States in 2001 by Simon & Schuster Books for Young Readers
an imprint of Simon & Schuster Children's Publishing Division, New York
First published in Great Britain in 2002 by Macmillan Children's Books
A division of Macmillan Publishers Limited
20 New Wharf Road, London N1 9RR
Basingstoke and Oxford
Associated companies throughout the world
www.panmacmillan.com

ISBN 0 333 98736 5 (HB)
ISBN 0 333 99288 1 (PB)

Text copyright © 2001 Marni McGee
Illustrations copyright © 2001 Sam Williams
Moral rights asserted

1 3 5 7 9 8 6 4 2

A CIP catalogue record for this book is available from the British Library.

Printed in Hong Kong

In loving memory of Claude U. Broach – preacher and poet, lover of life, singer of songs . . . writer, father, friend
– M. M.

For Brenda, Richard, and Becky
– S. W.

Sleepy cat.

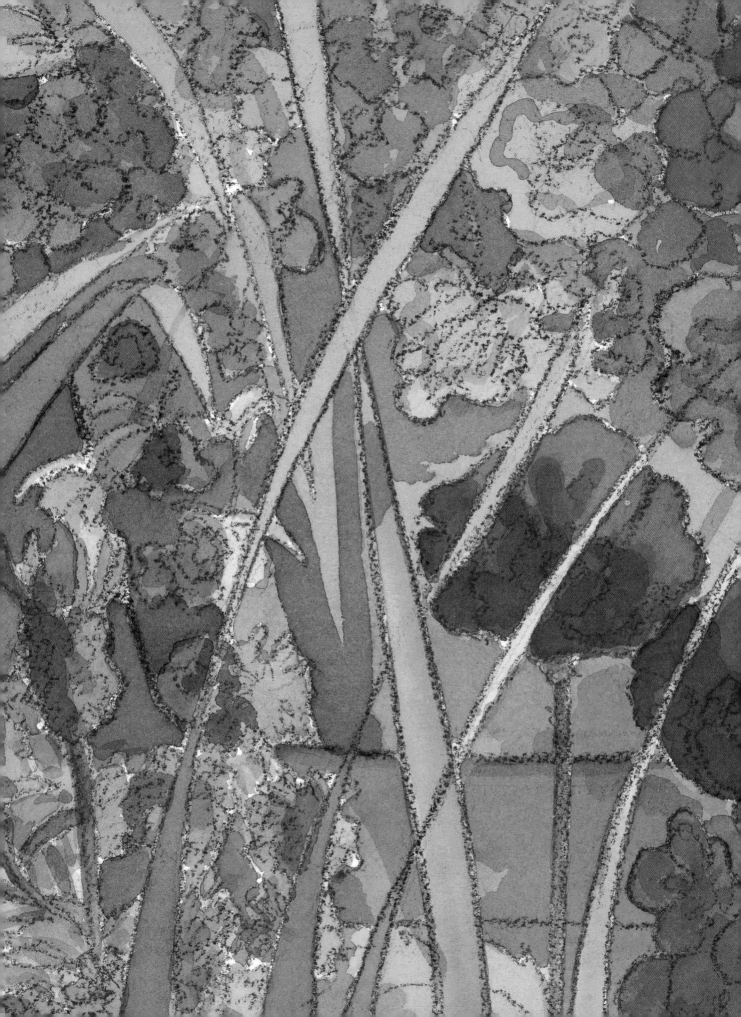

sleepy mouse.

Sleepy sounds inside the house.

Sleepy stair.

Sleepy chair.

Sleepy Daddy

rocks me there.

Sleepy bookcase.

Sleepy ball.

Sleepy mirror sees it all.

Sleepy star.
Sleepy tree.

Sleepy breeze blows in on me.

Sleepy story.
Sleepy sighs.

Sleepy Mum
will kiss my eyes.

Sleepy bed
with sleepy
bear.

My sleepy head

will soon be there.

Sleepy me,
sleeping tight.
Sleeping till the
morning light.

Sleepy,
sleepy me!